With love to
my sisters and brothers,
Thomas and Deborah Niehof,
Daniel and Lu Ann Kruis,
Beth Walburg, Timothy and Marcelle Walburg.

With humble thanks to Kathy Bieber,
for providing the initial research on Easter eggs,
and with deep gratitude to Bob Hudson,
Shelley Townsend-Hudson, and Susan Hill,
my first and best readers.

In memory of my great aunts Mae and Nell Goudzwaard.
I can't wait to see you again.

—LW

To my Mom,
for all the love and encouragement,
and for the many Easters spent together.
We missed you this year, and look forward to
seeing you on that Resurrection day!

—RC

ZONDERKIDZ

The Legends of Easter Treasury
This is a compilation of previously published stories:

The Legend of the Easter Egg (ISBN 978-0-310-73545-8)
Copyright © 1999 by Lori Walburg
Illustrations © 2013 by Richard Cowdrey

The Legend of the Easter Robin (ISBN 978-0-310-74964-6)
Copyright © 2010 by Dandi Daley Mackall
Illustrations © 2016 by Richard Cowdrey

The Legend of the Sand Dollar (978-0-310-74980-6)
Copyright © 2005 by Chris Auer
Illustrations © 2017 by Richard Cowdrey

Requests for information should be addressed to:
Zonderkidz, 3900 Sparks Drive SE, Grand Rapids, Michigan 49546

This edition: ISBN 978-0-310-75759-7 (hardcover)

Editor: Barbara Herndon
Art direction and design: Kris Nelson/StoryLook Design

Printed in China

17 18 19 20 21 22 23 /DSC/ 17 16 15 14 13 12 11 10 9 8 7 6 5 4 3 2 1

The Legend of the Easter Egg

The Inspirational Story of a Favorite Easter Tradition

WRITTEN BY Lori Walburg

ILLUSTRATED BY Richard Cowdrey

One April morning when the air was soft and sweet, a boy and his sister went outside to gather eggs.

"Easter's coming," the sister said. "Let's pretend we're hunting Easter eggs."

"What are Easter eggs?" the boy asked.

"Don't you remember?" the girl said.

He thought and thought, but the boy couldn't remember. He was going to ask again, but just then, the girl scared up a hen, squawking, from its nest in the grass. "Look!" she cried. Smiling, she held up a rosy brown egg.

That night, the boy woke to the sound of his name. "Thomas!" His mother's face bent over his. "Your sister is sick. Papa must take you away."

Thomas let his mother slip off his warm nightshirt. He held up his arms as she pulled a sweater over his head, and sat down when she tugged on his knickers. When she told him he could not see Lucy, he nodded. When Papa told him where he was taking him, he smiled.

But he was not really awake. He did not understand.

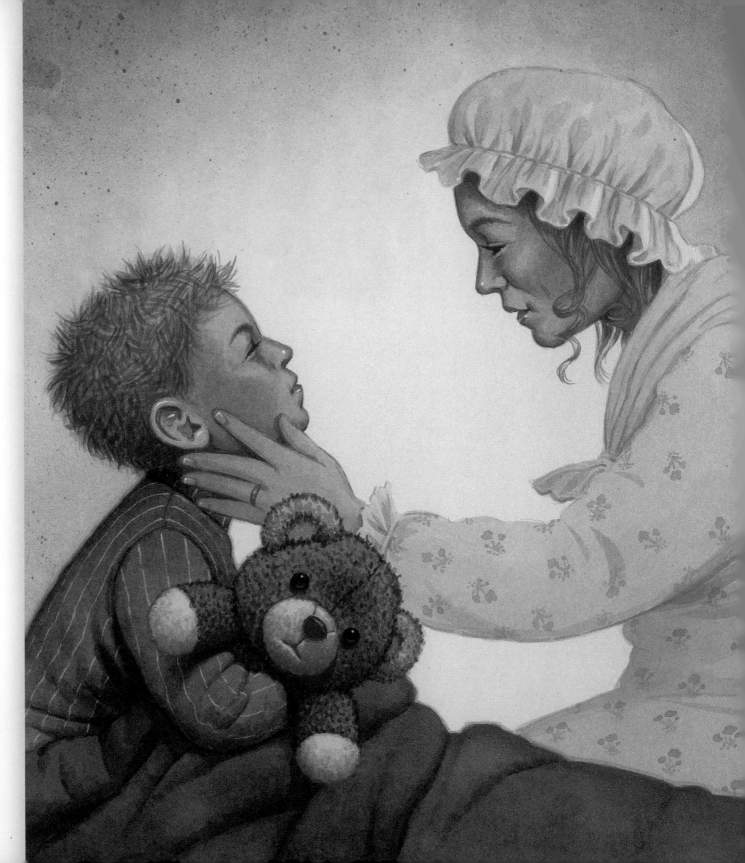

When he woke again, Thomas did not know where he was. His bedroom was gone. Mama, Papa, and Lucy were gone. But before he could even think about being scared, his eyes grew wide and he sat bolt upright.

Had he died? Was this heaven? Because all around him was candy. Long branches of licorice and tiny jeweled rock candy. Yellow, white, purple, and pink jelly beans. Marshmallow chicks and tiny chocolate eggs. He stood up very slowly.

"Morning, Thomas!" a familiar voice said.

It was John Sonneman. Thomas had come to stay with John and his new wife, Mary, at their candy store. Just as Papa had said.

All that long Wednesday, Thomas helped Mr. Sonneman in his store. He filled jars of candy. He weighed chocolate on the tippy scales and scrubbed the counter till it gleamed. All day, Mr. Sonneman let him eat smidgens of fudge and bits of broken peppermint sticks.

When he finished cleaning out the cookstove for Mrs. Sonneman, she looked at him and laughed. "Goodness, gracious!" she said. "You have ash on your face!"

With her thumb, she wiped him clean. He smiled. But inside, his heart felt as dusty and grey as the ash. His sister was sick. He couldn't be with her. And there was nothing he could do.

On Sunday after church, Thomas went outside to play. At the edge of a small stream, he broke off a young reed, put it between his two thumbs, and blew. "Squawk!"

"Ok-a-lay!" a red-winged blackbird sang in reply. Two swallows whirled overhead. "Cheer! Cheer!" they cried.

Suddenly, Thomas threw the reed at them, then snatched up pebbles and threw them too. A robin cocked his head, peering at him with one eye. "Tut-tut," it chided.

"Silly birds," Thomas muttered as he turned away.

More days passed. Thomas learned that Lucy had scarlet fever. A red rash covered her body. Her face burned with fever. Every night at dinner, John Sonneman prayed for her to get well.

Sometimes, Mary Sonneman felt Thomas's forehead. He wished he could be sick too. But his body was white and healthy. And his face, cool and dry.

On Thursday, Mary sent him out to trade for eggs. When he returned, his shoes and socks were caked in mud.

"Spring!" Mary laughed. "So beautiful and so messy at the same time." Kneeling, she took off his shoes and socks, then cleaned his feet in a pail of warm water. The water tickled his toes, and for the first time in days, he giggled.

Friday dawned bleak and cold. At noon, the stores closed. And everyone went to church.

Thomas listened to the story of Jesus' death. The minister talked for a long time. "Though your sins be as scarlet, they shall be as white as snow," he said.

While the adults shared bread and wine, Thomas slowly ate a white peppermint. Then he ate a pink peppermint. For a while, he forgot Lucy. Snuggled under John Sonneman's arm, he fell asleep.

He awoke to bedlam. Lanterns and candles flashed against the dark afternoon. Overhead, something terrible battered at the roof of the church. Thomas gripped John Sonneman's hand as the townspeople crowded at the doorway, peering out.

"Hail," they said.

High above, the church bell swung wildly, pelted by icy pebbles. As the afternoon passed and the hail turned to freezing rain, the bell fell silent. Frozen.

That night, as Mary Sonneman tucked him into bed, Thomas asked, "Is Lucy going to die, just like Jesus did?"

"Shh," said Mary. "She will not die. She is just very sick."

"I want to see her!" he cried. "I want to be with her!"

"Soon," Mary said. "She is almost well. You will see her soon."

She put her hand into her pocket and pulled out a small chocolate egg. "Here is your first Easter egg," she said. "Sunday is Easter. On Easter, you will see your sister again."

Thomas remembered hunting for eggs. And he remembered the question that Lucy had never answered. "What are Easter eggs?" he asked again.

Mary pressed the small egg into his palm and wrapped his fingers around it.

"Three days after Jesus died, early on Sunday morning, some women came to Jesus' tomb,"
she said. "They were sad. They had come to mourn Jesus' death. But when they arrived,
they saw the stone had been rolled away from the tomb!"

Thomas held up the egg. "Did the stone look like this?"

Mary laughed. "Yes, only much bigger and much heavier!"
Mary continued, "Then an angel came and told the women that Jesus was not
there. He was alive! Filled with joy and fear, the women ran to tell the other
disciples. And that was the first Easter."

"But why do we have Easter eggs?" Thomas asked.

Mary explained, "Just as a chick breaks out of an egg, so had Jesus broken free of the tomb of death. Easter eggs remind us that Jesus conquered death and gives us eternal life."

"So Lucy won't die?"

Mary shook her head. "Someday she will. And you will too. But if you believe in Jesus, you will see each other again in heaven. That is the promise and joy of Easter!"

She tucked the blanket under his chin. "Remember," she said, "believe in Jesus. Hope and pray. That's what you can do for your sister. All right?"

"Okay," Thomas agreed.

All day Saturday, Thomas stayed inside and colored eggs. Outside, the freezing rain fell. But inside, he stood near the glowing cookstove, dipping eggs. As he plunged the cool white eggs into the warm red dye, he thought of Lucy's fever. He remembered the story of the Easter egg. And for the first time in his life, he prayed. All by himself.

Very early Easter morning, before anyone woke up, Thomas filled a basket with colored eggs and slipped out the door. As he walked, the sun came up. And all around him, the world began to sparkle.

The twigs on the trees and the tiny buds sparkled. The stubbled wheat fields and the long, waving reeds sparkled. Even the ice-bent daffodils and crushed violets, the trampled crocuses and the battered hyacinths glittered like jewels in the muddy farmyards. Thomas caught his breath. He had never seen anything so beautiful.

He passed the cemetery. The gravestones, too, twinkled in their shining gowns of ice.

And the church bell began to ring.

When he got home,
Thomas bounded up the
stairs to Lucy's room.
Finally, he would see her.
Finally, he would tell her.
Of the story of the Easter
egg. Of his faith in Jesus.
His hope for new life. And
the love they shared that
would never, ever, end.

Traditions and Symbols of Lent and Easter

The forty days before Easter are traditionally known as Lent. Lent begins on Ash Wednesday. In the Old Testament, God's people put ashes on themselves when they were deeply sorry for their sins. On Ash Wednesday, Christians receive the mark of ashes on their foreheads to remind them of their sins and their need to repent.

On Maundy Thursday, Christians remember Jesus' Last Supper with his disciples. They break bread to remind them of Christ's broken body. And they drink wine to remind them of Christ's shed blood. Sometimes, they will wash each other's feet, to remind them to serve and love each other, as Christ loved his disciples and served them by washing their feet.

On Good Friday, Christians remember Christ's death. Through Scripture readings, sermons, prayers, and hymns, they worship Jesus and commemorate his suffering and death.

Finally, on Easter Sunday, Christians celebrate Christ's resurrection. The egg, an ancient symbol of new life, has become for Christians a symbol of the resurrection. Through the gift of Easter eggs, Christians remind each other that through Christ's resurrection, they too will conquer death and receive the gift of eternal life.

For Granny and Katy
—DDM

To Louis Koenig, thank you.
—RC

The Legend of the Easter Robin

An Easter Story of Compassion and Faith

WRITTEN BY Dandi Daley Mackall

ILLUSTRATED BY Richard Cowdrey

"What's the matter with her, Gran?" Tressa and her grandmother had watched two robins carry twigs, cat hair, and string to build a nest on Gran's window ledge. Now the bird wiggled, tail twitching while its red-orange breast rose and fell.

"That mama's just molding her nest for a good fit," Gran answered.

But Tressa worried. It was still two weeks until Easter. A million things could go wrong when a robin tried to nest this early.

The next day, Tressa
ran straight to Gran's after
school. Gran showed her
the surprise. In the center
of the nest lay one perfect
egg, the color of a spring
sky. The father robin sat on
a branch nearby, guarding
his family. Tressa spotted
raccoon tracks below and
a blue jay eyeing the nest.
"Gran, how are we going to
keep the egg safe?"

"We'll have to leave that
one to the Creator," Gran
said.

Over the next three days, the robin laid three more eggs. Tressa watched the mother robin nudge her eggs before huddling onto them again.

"Turning her eggs keeps them from freezing," Gran explained. "See that bare spot on her red breast? God made her so she could warm her babies through that brood patch."

Tressa hoped that would be enough.

The day before Easter, a cold snap hit. Frost laced the windowpane and whitened the nest. "Now the eggs will never hatch, Gran!" Tressa cried.

"We'll have to trust the one who watches the sparrow and robins," Gran said. "Now come with me. It's about time we saw to some other eggs."

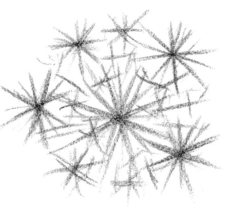

Gran got some eggs from her refrigerator. She poked tiny holes in the top and bottom of each egg. Then she blew the gooey insides into a bowl, leaving the shells in one piece. "I'll show you how to make oschter-foggel, Easter birds. It's an old Pennsylvania Dutch tradition I learned from my granny."

Tressa blew half-heartedly on her egg. All she could think about were the real eggs outside in the cold.

Gran dipped her egg into blue-tinted water. When she lifted the shell from the dye, it was robin's egg blue.

Tressa knew Gran—and God—cared as much about those baby robins as she did. And Gran wasn't worried. Tressa tried blowing out her egg again. This time it worked.

Gran grinned over at her. "Since we have robins on our minds, how would you like to hear the legend behind the robin's red breast?"

Tressa dipped her egg into the dye while Gran began her story.

Around two thousand years ago, a plain brown robin was flying over Jerusalem when he heard angry shouts from the streets below. Swooping down to see what the fuss was about, he caught sight of a man, beaten and bent under the weight of a wooden cross.

I know this man, thought the robin. All earth's creatures, except humans, recognized Jesus— the Creator-God come to earth.

At first the robin thought he saw a nest on Jesus' head.
But when he soared closer, he understood. The "nest"
was a cruel crown of thorns.
I must help the master!
thought the robin.
But what could he do?

Jesus stumbled as a whip snapped. He fell, and the
thorny crown dug into his head. The robin, filled
with compassion, flew at the crown and tried
to knock it off Jesus' head. But the crown
wouldn't budge.

It was then that the robin noticed one long thorn sticking into Jesus' forehead. The bird gathered its strength, grabbed the thorn in its beak, and tugged.

The thorn gave way. And as it came out, a drop of Jesus' blood fell onto the robin's breast, staining it red from that day to this.

"Ever since," Gran said, "the robin's red breast reminds us of Christ's sacrifice and how much he cares. The robin's song is the first sign of spring, helping us remember that after Christ died, he rose again on that first Easter."

Tressa insisted they color the rest of the eggs robin's egg blue. Gran taught her how to cut wings, heads, and tails for the Easter birds they'd hang from trees in the morning.

When Tressa woke up on Easter morning, she ran to Gran's to hang their Easter birds. As she tiptoed beneath the robins' nest, something crunched under her shoe. Jagged chips of blue shell lay scattered over the ground.

"Gran!" she cried as she burst into the house. "The eggs! They're broken!"

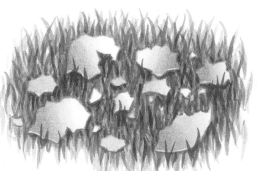

Gran called Tressa up to her room. "Take a look."

Under the mother robin's wing sat four scrawny baby robins, eyes closed and mouths wide open. "They're alive!" Tressa exclaimed. She watched the daddy robin drop bits of food into the babies' mouths.

"God takes care of his creatures," Gran whispered.

Through the windowpane, Tressa could see the robins' red breasts, bright against the sunrise. She was sorry she'd ever doubted God's care. From then on, whenever she saw a robin or felt worried, she'd think of the legend. And she'd remember all Jesus went through that first Easter season.

"Thank you," she prayed, "for the robins ... and for Jesus."

Outside the wind howled, but the robins' joyful chirping came through loud and true. To Tressa, it sounded like they were wishing her a happy Easter.

She answered them. "Happy Easter to you too!"

About the Legend of the Easter Robin

The legend of the robin's red breast is an old Pennsylvania Dutch tale. The point of the legend is a celebration of the robin's compassion and of Christ's sacrifice.

The Pennsylvania Dutch are also given credit for bringing egg coloring to the United States, and for being the first to decorate trees with Easter birds. We can use traditions and symbols to strengthen our faith and help us remember.

- The robin is a sign of spring, and it can remind us of Christ's love for us, his death, and resurrection.

- Birds' nests help us remember Christ's crown of thorns. The first Easter baskets were made to look like nests.

- The robin's red breast is a symbol of Christ's suffering and love.

- Easter eggs remind us of our new life in Christ.

This book is dedicated to all six of my wonderful children ...
"a shout of joy comes in the morning."

—CA

To John for all of the encouragement ... Thanks Barney!

—RC

The Legend of the Sand Dollar

An Inspirational Story of Hope for Easter

WRITTEN BY Chris Auer

ILLUSTRATED BY Richard Cowdrey

Why can't Mom and Dad take us to the beach?" Kerry sniffled.

"It's only two days," whispered Margaret, "and they'll come get us on Easter morning."

Kerry tried not to cry. Every few years her family went to Aunt Jane's house near the beach. *I'll just think about playing with Cousin Jack,* she told herself. *I'll just think about the ocean.*

But her tears still fell as the bus took her farther and farther away from her mom and dad.

Early the next morning at Aunt Jane's, Kerry went out to look at the boats on the river.

Kerry still missed her parents, but soon she heard the *putt-putt-putt* of an engine coming toward her from upstream. Cousin Jack!

"Kerry!" Jack hollered.

"What do you think about my new boat?"

"It's not very big," she called back.

"Then it's perfect for you!" He took her hand as she climbed on board.

The river opened to the wide bay.

"Hang on!" Jack yelled. Suddenly, the ocean lay before them, as broad as the sky. A small island appeared in the distance.

Waves lapped against the shore as Jack beached the boat.

"What's this?" Kerry called, holding up a round object.

"That's a sand dollar," Jack answered.

"A sand dollar?" Kerry cried. "This isn't money!"

"Right," said Jack. "It's a starfish that used to live in the ocean."

"How do they get here?" Kerry asked.

"When the tide goes out, it leaves sand dollars behind," Jack said.

"Why are they called dollars?" she asked.

"Real dollars used to be round," said Jack, "and they were made of silver. But sand dollars have value too."

"Then I guess we're rich," Kerry teased.

"In a way," he answered. "The sand dollar tells a story—the greatest story of all."

"Can you see the Easter lily on that side?
It's like a trumpet saying, 'Jesus is alive!'"

"Now look in the middle of the lily. There's the star from the East that led wise men to Christ. We remember Jesus' birth on this side too. See the Christmas flower?"

"Both sides of the sand dollar tell the Easter story.
See the four nail holes—and a fifth hole made by
a spear? These remind us that Jesus died for us."

"Now hold out your hand," said Jack, "and watch very carefully." He broke open one of the sand dollars, and five white shapes fluttered down.

"See the doves? This is the new life—the promise of Easter. As Jesus lives again, so can we. And these doves remind us to spread his promise and this hope to all people."

"Oh, no!" Kerry cried. "We dropped them!"

Jack wasn't worried. "The high tide will leave more, over and over. And I have a whole bucketful back home."

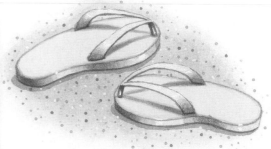

As the tide rushed ashore again, Jack helped Kerry back into the boat, pushed it off the beach, and jumped inside.

The boat crested the top of each wave, hung in the air, then swooped down like a ride on a roller coaster.

But all the way back, Kerry could only think about the sand dollar and how valuable it really was.

That night, the moon rose full across the water.

"You know what?" asked Jack. "Your parents aren't that far away—like the moon and the tide."

"But the moon is far away from the ocean," said Kerry.

"They're still connected," Jack explained. "The moon's gravity is what pulls the tide high."

"From that far away?"

"That's how the tide works."

"Like how God can remind us that he is close too," whispered Kerry, thinking of the sand dollar.

The next morning, Kerry put a sand dollar into her sister's hands.

"Happy Easter, Margaret," she said.

"Thanks, Kerry!"

Kerry smiled and asked, "Do you see the Easter lily?"

"An Easter lily?"

"Yeah, and inside there are little doves. I'll tell you the whole story."

As they waited for their parents, Kerry shared the good news with her sister.

Soon Margaret smiled too.

All about Sand Dollars

Sand dollar is the name for a marine animal that is related to the starfish. Sand dollars have flat, rigid, disk-shaped shells made of interlocked plates just beneath their skin.

Living sand dollars are fuzzy and brown or pinkish. They burrow in sand, feeding on small organic particles. Just their skeletons— or shells—wash onto beaches.

Only collect sand dollars that are no longer alive. They look like white coins and are about 1–4 inches (approx. 2.5–10 cm) in diameter. Sand dollars are easiest to find at low tide, along the edge of the receding water. The sand washes away from the buried shells as a wave goes out, and the next wave covers them with sand again.

In North America, people who live along the coastline often recite this popular poem about sand dollars:

There's a pretty little legend
That I would like to tell
Of the birth and death of Jesus
Found in this lowly shell.

If you examine closely,
You'll see that you find here
Four nail holes and a fifth one
Made by a Roman's spear.

On one side; the Easter lily.
It's center is the star
That appeared unto the shepherds
And led them from afar.

The Christmas poinsettia
Etched on the other side
Reminds us of his birthday,
Our happy Christmastide.

Now break the center open,
And here you will release
The five doves awaiting
To spread good will and peace.

This simple little symbol
Christ left for you and me
To help us spread his gospel
Through all eternity.

–Author Unknown